D0286500

This notebook belongs to :
